Ex-Library: Friends of
Lake County Public Library

SHLEMAZEL
AND THE
REMARKABLE
SPOON OF POHOST

SHLEMAZEL
AND THE
REMARKABLE
SPOON OF POHOST

by Ann Redisch Stampler

Illustrated by Jacqueline M. Cohen

Clarion Books • New York

The author is grateful to Miriam Koral, director of the California Institute for Yiddish Culture
and Language, for her help. Thanks also to Ron Coleman, research librarian,
and Michlean Amir, reference archivist,
at the United States Holocaust Memorial Museum.

Clarion Books
a Houghton Mifflin Company imprint
215 Park Avenue South, New York, NY 10003
Text copyright © 2006 by Ann Redisch Stampler
Illustrations copyright © 2006 by Jacqueline M. Cohen

The illustrations were executed in watercolor.
The text was set in 16-point Berkeley Book.

www.houghtonmifflinbooks.com

Printed in China

Library of Congress Cataloging-in-Publication Data

Stampler, Ann Redisch.
Shlemazel and the remarkable spoon of Pohost / by Ann Redisch Stampler ;
illustrated by Jacqueline M. Cohen.
p. cm. Summary: A retelling of an Eastern European tale in which Shlemazel,
the laziest man in town, is tricked into believing that the lucky spoon given to him by a neighbor
will bring him fortune and fame, if it is used in the right way.
ISBN-13: 978-0-618-36959-1
ISBN-10: 0-618-36959-7
[1. Luck—Folklore. 2. Laziness—Folklore. 3. Folklore.] I. Cohen, Jacqueline M., ill.
II. Title.
PZ8.1.S7865Shl 2006   398.2—dc22   2005023602

SCP 10 9 8 7 6 5 4 3 2 1

For my husband, Rick, with love
—A.R.S.

For Barb, Nancy, and Vaughan
—J.M.C.

On the rickety porch of a crooked old house in the tumbledown village of Pohost sat Shlemazel, whittling a stick. There Shlemazel sat until birds nested in his hair in summer and snow filled his pockets in winter.

"Shlemazel is the laziest man in Pohost," complained Yussel the tailor.

"Lazy-shmazy," said Shlemazel. "I am not lazy. I'm unlucky."

"Everyone else works from sunup to sundown," said Yussel, "while you sit on the same stool, scraping the same dry stick with a knife as dull as a toenail."

"A man with my bad luck can't use a sharp knife," explained Shlemazel. "A sharp knife would jump from my unlucky hand and cut off all my buttons."

8

"Shlemazel is as lazy as a cat full of cream. He'll never work," sighed Chaim the cobbler.

"Work-shmurk," protested Shlemazel. "Why, if I left this porch to go to work before sunrise, my candle would slip from my unlucky fingers and start a great fire that would burn the whole village to ash."

"Poor Shlemazel," said Moshke the tinker, a hardworking fellow with three sons, a plump wife, and five yellow chickens. "Sitting on his porch day after day, he will never know the pleasure of a good day's work, or find a wife, or do one single good deed. I wish we could help him."

"Help him?" snorted Yussel. "Why, you'd have to chase him with a bag of bees to move him half an inch."

"No, no!" cried Moshke. "We'd just have to convince him he's lucky. How hard could that be?"

"Once an idea flies into Shlemazel's head, he doesn't let it go for years," replied Yussel.

"Pancakes and honey will rain from the sky before Shlemazel changes his ways," said Chaim.

"Pearls will grow in turnips before Shlemazel finds his luck," Yussel concluded with a laugh.

"You'll see," said Moshke. "You'll see."

Moshke thought and thought until a plan was simmering in his brain. Then he reached into his wagon and pulled out a spoon. It was tarnished and pockmarked and green around the edges.

"Beho-o-o-old!" howled Moshke, spinning the spoon and waving it over his head. "Behold!"

"That is a very big spoon," observed Shlemazel.

"It's no ordinary spoon," said Moshke. "This is the amazing, remarkable spoon of Pohost."

"Ohhhh," said Shlemazel. "The amazing, remarkable spoon of Pohost? What does it do?"

"It finds luck," confided Moshke. "I haul this spoon from town to town, sharpening knives and mending kettles all week long— and I'm as lucky as can be! I come home to a Sabbath feast with zlotys in my pocket."

"I wish I had such a spoon, so I could find my luck," Shlemazel said.

"Your life would be filled up with blessings and surprises if you found your luck," Moshke agreed.

"How I want that lucky spoon," said Shlemazel.

"With this amazing spoon, a man can find all the treasure he'll ever need," said Moshke.

"How I *need* that lucky spoon," moaned Shlemazel.

"Take it!" cried Moshke, grinning. "You need it more than I do. With this amazing, remarkable spoon, I guarantee you'll find your luck."

Shlemazel grabbed for the spoon. "But tell me, Moshke," he said, "where should I take this spoon to look for my luck?"

Moshke pressed the spoon against his head, as if it could send messages directly to his brain. "Mmm," he murmured. "Yes, I see. . . ." He pointed to a field littered with rocks and weeds, bottomless buckets, and discarded shoes. "Dig over there! Your luck is underneath the ground."

Shlemazel gasped. "That's the poretz's field," he said. "If I disturb it, he'll pluck me like a duck. He'll take whatever luck I find and keep it for himself."

"The poretz has a warehouse full of gold and land past the horizon," said Moshke, putting the spoon in Shlemazel's hand. "What would such a fellow want with one little Shlemazel's luck?"

"You're right!" Shlemazel cried.

Clutching the spoon, Shlemazel ran to the field, where he zigzagged up and down,

spooning great clumps of dirt and hurling rubbish into messy mounds.

He pulled weeds and rolled rocks and dug furrows all week long. He didn't stop to watch the village girls wandering to the well, not even pretty Chaya Massel.

When the poretz heard that Shlemazel had dug up his field, he rode to the edge of the village to see for himself. Sure enough, his useless plot of rocks and rubbish was now neatly plowed brown soil. "Why have you plowed my field, silly Shlemazel?" he asked.

"Bad luck," replied Shlemazel, too tired even to be scared of the poretz. "I am so unlucky that even with this amazing, remarkable spoon, I didn't find a single scrap of luck."

"I'll give you luck!" boomed the poretz, tossing a sack of coins into the field. "For when I sell the turnips I shall grow in this field, they'll bring me quite a bit of luck."

When Moshke pushed his wagon home to Pohost that Friday afternoon, he was astonished at the sight of the poretz's plowed field and Shlemazel with the zlotys spread before him on the ground.

"I see that you have found your luck," said Moshke.

"Found-shmound," Shlemazel grumbled, gathering up the zlotys. "All week, I searched under the ground for my luck, but all I have to show for it is this handful of coins."

"But just look at all those zlotys," marveled Moshke.

"Zlotys-shlotys," groused Shlemazel, limping back to his rickety porch. "I want luck, not zlotys."

"Don't give up," urged Moshke. "Finding luck is hard work. If it were easy, beggars would be princes and crows would fly straight to the kingdom of worms."

"You're right," declared Shlemazel. "I'll dig up everything in all Pohost to find my luck."

"Wait!" yelled Moshke, pressing the spoon against his forehead. All he could think of was the poor old miller, who needed help more than anyone else in Pohost. "Hmm," said Moshke. "Yes, I see. . . . Your luck is not under the *ground*. It is under the *grain* that is *ground* at the mill."

Shlemazel hurried to the mill, where the miller was grinding the poretz's wagonfuls of grain into flour all by himself. "How can one little Shlemazel with a rusty spoon help me?" the miller sighed, watching as the new-ground flour burst from the chute and cascaded into mountains on the floor.

"This is the amazing, remarkable spoon of Pohost," declared Shlemazel. "You'll see!"

When the miller took the padlock from the great mill door after the Sabbath, Shlemazel raced inside. He spooned flour into sacks and stacked them from floor to ceiling all week long.

One morning, he heard the doorbell clang. There stood the baker's daughter, Chaya Massel, come to buy some flour.

"What are you doing here, you ghost of a Shlemazel?" Chaya Massel asked kindly.

"I am looking for my luck with the amazing, remarkable spoon of Pohost," he replied.

"Well, if you find luck, I could surely do with some." Chaya smiled sweetly. "For when I think of all the bread and cake I have to bake, I want to sleep right where I stand."

"I'd rather sleep than shovel flour," Shlemazel said.
"But I must find my luck."

"Have you heard?" Yussel called to Moshke as the tinker pushed his wagon home on Friday. "Shlemazel did the miller's work all by himself, all week!"

"The miller tried to hire him," marveled Chaim. "And when the blacksmith heard how hard Shlemazel worked, he tried to hire him, too!"

Moshke raced to Shlemazel's porch. "What luck!" he exclaimed. "I hear the miller wants to hire you."

"Miller-shmiller," snapped Shlemazel. "All week long, I spooned a flood of flour into giant sacks. But did I find my luck? No, I did not! And now everybody wants to hire me and make me work some more."

"But if you were a miller or a blacksmith, you could find a wife," Moshke pointed out.

"Wife-shmife," grumbled Shlemazel. "Where is the luck you promised me? It's not under the ground, and it's not in the grain."

Quickly, Moshke pressed the spoon against his head. All he could think of was poor Chaya Massel, baking for the whole village all by herself. "Mmm," he murmured. "Yes, I see! . . . Shlemazel, think how grain grows. It roots under the *ground* and then the miller *grinds* the *grain*, and this makes *flour*."

"Flour-shmour," muttered Shlemazel. "Where's my luck?"

"Flour becomes the baker's batter!" Moshke said. "Chaya Massel buys the flour and takes it to the bakery to bake in cake. Your luck is in the baker's batter!"

"You're right!" Shlemazel cried.

Shlemazel skipped all the way to Chaya Massel's door. "I am here to stir the batter with the amazing, remarkable spoon of Pohost," he called to her.

"I won't turn down an offer of help, however strange," said Chaya Massel. "But we don't work on Friday night. Shlemazel, would you care to share the Sabbath meal?"

Shlemazel followed his nose toward savory tsimmes, and soon he saw how Chaya Massel's face shone in the candlelight.

The next night, Chaya Massel welcomed Shlemazel gladly at the bakery.

"I'm ready to stir the batter!" cried Shlemazel, waving the amazing, remarkable spoon over his head.

"Of course," said Chaya Massel. "But first, perhaps, you'll let me show you how to make it." She taught Shlemazel how to crack the eggs and sift the flour, how to knead the dough and braid the challah. Shlemazel found himself thinking that it would be pleasant to stand beside Chaya Massel, stirring great bowls full of batter all week long, summer and winter.

And this is how it happened that when Moshke returned in the
long shadows that Friday, only the first chill wind of autumn was
complaining on Shlemazel's porch.

"I don't know how you did it, Moshke," whispered Yussel the
tailor. "Shlemazel is now the luckiest man alive. He is to marry
Chaya Massel, and she's made a baker out of him."

"It's true," whispered Chaim the cobbler. "The poretz
himself is to give them a cow."

Moshke burst through the bakery door, whistling like a bird. "Mazel tov, Shlemazel!" he cried. "I see that you have found your luck."

"Mazel-shmazel," said Shlemazel. "I can tell you everything that's in this batter, but for certain, there is no luck whatsoever!"

"You are to marry Chaya Massel," chortled Moshke. "The sweetest girl in all Pohost. What luck!"

"*Luck?*" asked Shlemazel. "Chaya Massel marries me because she loves me, even though I have no luck at all."

"But the poretz will give you a cow at your wedding!" cried Moshke. "Is that not luck?"

Shlemazel shrugged. "The poretz gives me a cow because I plowed his field and saved his flour. Where is the luck in that?"

"I tell you, you have found your luck," insisted Moshke. "You were once the poorest, laziest, silliest man in Pohost, and now you are a baker."

"Bakers must rise with the moon and labor for hours before breakfast," said Shlemazel. "That is work, not luck."

Moshke shook his head, sat down on a three-legged stool in the corner of the bakery, and sighed deeply.

"Don't worry, Moshke," said Shlemazel. He laid the amazing, remarkable spoon of Pohost in Moshke's lap. "A fellow with a sweet wife and a milk cow and a baker's bowl does not need a great deal of luck. For even though I have no luck, I am perfectly happy without it."

Author's Note

When my grandmother left the Eastern European village of Pohost (puh-HOST) for New England in the early part of the twentieth century, she brought with her an immigrant's determination and the unshakable belief that in her adopted land great things could be accomplished. The optimism and self-sufficiency that helped make her tough and resilient, that propelled her across the ocean and into hard work and success once she got here, also permeated her stories. This traditional Shlemazel tale, which she told me in her accented English, is no exception.

What I love about this story is not just that Moshke the tinker tricks Shlemazel (meaning, literally, "without luck") into becoming a mensch, but how he does so. The tasks Shlemazel must perform to "find his luck" are preparing the soil to be planted, then helping to grind grain into flour, and finally baking the grain into bread for his community. Along the way, Shlemazel develops something of a work ethic, begins to celebrate the Sabbath, and finds love and a good woman to marry. He becomes a self-respecting and worthy individual through actions that bind him to his community and his heritage. And as the transformed Shlemazel himself points out, none of this required a bit of luck.

My grandmother's first name, Ida, was assigned to her at Ellis Island when her original name could not be pronounced easily in English. It pleases me to give my grandmother's real name, Chaya Massel, to the baker who marries Shlemazel, in this tale that marries the beliefs of the Old World and the New.

Glossary

challah (HAH-luh) A braided egg bread traditionally eaten at the Sabbath dinner

mazel tov (MAH-z'l tuv) Literally "good luck," used to express congratulations

mensch (MENSH) Literally "a person," with connotations of goodness, trustworthiness, responsibility, and sympathy

poretz (POR-ets) A wealthy landowner

shlemazel (shluh-MAH-z'l) A very unlucky person

tsimmes (TZIH-mus) A fragrant stew of fruits and vegetables

zlotys (ZLO-tiss) The basic unit of money in Poland, the root words suggesting something golden and shining